Should You Be Laughing at This?

Hugleikur Dagsson

Should You Be Laughing at This?

HARPER

An Imprint of HarperCollins*Publishers*
www.harpercollins.com

HarperCollins books may be purchased for educational, business, or sales promotional use. For information please write: Special Markets Department, HarperCollins Publishers, 10 East 53rd Street, New York, NY 10022.

First published in Iceland in 2006 as *Avoid Us* by JPV Publishers.

Published in Great Britain in 2006 by Michael Joseph, an imprint of Penguin Books.

FIRST U.S. EDITION

Library of Congress Cataloging-in-Publication Data is available upon request.

ISBN: 978-0-06-128489-2

ISBN-10: 0-06-128489-0

11   OFF/RRD   10   9   8   7   6   5   4

Prologue

Finally this book has been made available for the non-Icelandic reader. In Iceland it is a famous good book. It contains the bulk of three small books originally published separately for greater profit. Books have been written in Iceland for more than eighty years and in Iceland, reading them is our favourite pastime. The harsh climate becomes soft and cozy when you read a book.

Hugleikur's books have been a huge success in Iceland, and why shouldn't they be "the talk of the town" elsewhere as well? If there ever were a capturer of moments such as our Hully, a wanderer better equipped, a prophesy sung in higher notes; let that selfsame know that he is a true warrior. The success of Hully's books in Iceland spawned a theatrical outcry of his rage when in October 2005 a play was premiered starring some of Iceland's most prominent acting students. They took to the stage and did their very best. Hully has been the talk of the town ever since.

I am in love with a demon. Hully has through his simple artwork built a bridge between the educated artist's outlets and the pretty public. A bridge over troubled water. The masses in Iceland have taken to Hully's books like mice to cheese and the educated artist is by no means less enthralled.

Hully's humour may be local but on the other hand it may also be universal. Only time will tell.

Fridrik Solnes, electrician.

FUCK ME

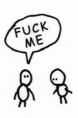

IT BURNS
WC

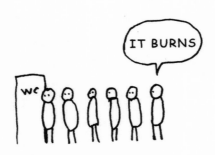

AAARGH, YOU ARE SUCH AN UGLY AND RETARDED LITTLE BITCH!!!!
YOU SMELL LIKE SHIT, MOM, AND DADDY HATES YOU!!!

LET ME HOLD THE BABY. IT CLEARLY FINDS YOUR PRESENCE UNBEAR-ABLE
WAAAH
WAAAAH

M

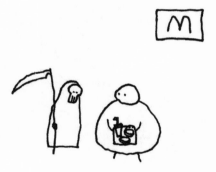

HI HON, WE'RE HAVING MEAT STEW FOR DINNER
WHERE ARE THE CHILDREN?

OH JA KLAUS!
AHH!
HEY DAD. ARE MY BOYS WITH YOU?

SON, WHEN YOU GROW UP, YOU WILL MARRY ME AND BEAR MY CHILDREN
YES FATHER

SO YOU'RE THE ONE WHO'S MARRYING MY DAUGHTER! HAHAHAHA! I GUESS I HAVE TO GIVE YA A GOOD SPANKING NOW! HAHAHAHAHA!
HEH
JOEY, HE'S SERIOUS.

HONEY, COULD YOU GO TO THE STORE FOR ME? I NEED SOME MILK, EGGS AND A BOTTLE OF TOMATO JUICE.
MILK, EGGS AND A BOTTLE OF TEQUILA! SEE YA!!

BROOM...SHITFUCK... ...BEEP-BEEP...SATAN'S COCK AND CUM... ...BROOOM!!...
KIDS, WHY DON'T YOU PLAY WITH ANDREW? HE'S A LITTLE SHY.

JEEZ! YOU'VE BEEN WATCHING TV ALL DAY!
WHAT DO YOU MEAN?
AND WHO ARE YOU?

IS THAT MY VOMIT YOU'RE DRINKING?
glug glug

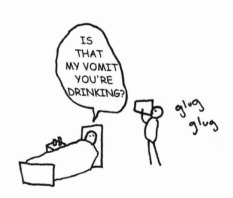

SAY HELLO TO HOWARD, KIDS! HE'S YOUR NEW NANNY!
GRRR GRRR

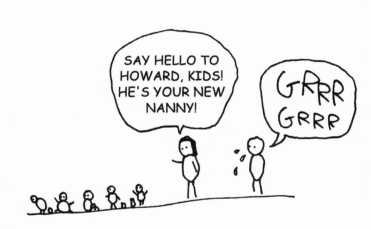

SCREAM FOR ME, FAGGOT!!
KR

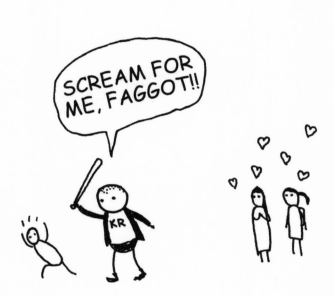

TRA LA LA
HEH... GUYS, YOU SHOULDN'T DANCE ON YOUR GRANDAD

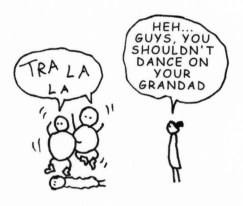

I MARRIED MY SISTER!!

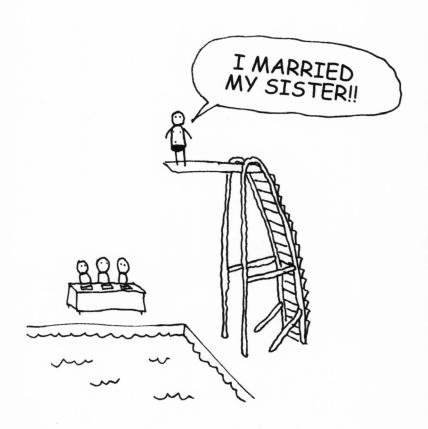

WHAT DO YOU WANT FOR CHRIST-MAS, MY LOVE?
A DIVORCE AND A BLACK LOVER, PLEASE.

STOP LISTEN-ING TO OTHER PEOPLE AND DO WHAT YOU WANNA DO FOR A CHANGE!
YOU GOT IT!

IS THAT A THIRD LEG, OR IS YOUR DICK JUST THAT BIG?
THAT'S FOR ME TO KNOW, AND YOU TO FIND OUT, BABY!

GOSH, I'M PRETTY! UNLIKE MY TROLL OF A DAUGHTER!
I'M STANDING BEHIND YOU, MOTHER.

SOLID!
SOLID AS A ROCK!
I CAN'T WAIT TO INTRODUCE YOU TO MY HUSBAND...

WHOA! GRANDAD'S LONG DEAD! I DIDN'T EVEN NOTICE!
HA HA HA

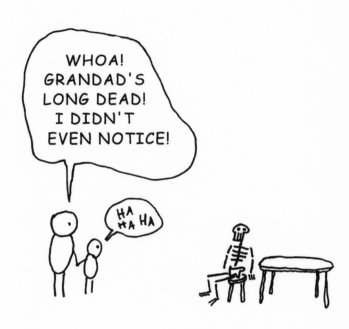

AND THIS IS MY CAT, SNUGGLES
THAT'S NOT A CAT. THAT'S A PIECE OF SHIT.

WHOEVER FINISHES THE TEST LAST, HAS TO DANCE NAKED IN FRONT OF THE CLASS

HONEY, WE NEED TO TALK.
CATS
GAY PRIDE
IT'S RAINING MEN
PLAY GIRL

MOMMY, CAN YOU WIPE ME, PLEASE?
...YOU ARE SO DISGUSTING.

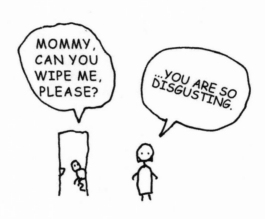

MARRY YOU? BUT YOUR PENIS IS LIKE, SO VERY, VERY, VERY, VERY, VERY, VERY, VERY, VERY, VERY, VERY SMALL!

WHY HELLO THERE MOTHER! I WAS FUCKING MY BROTHER JUST NOW...

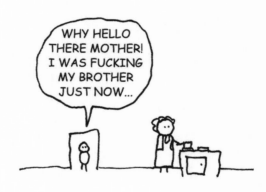

HA HA LOOK AT ME, BABY!

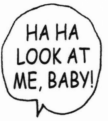

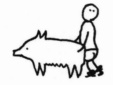

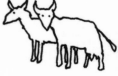

AAAH! AAA AAAH!
AUSTIN! WHAT ARE YOU DOING TO YOUR SON!?!

...AND BRING ME A HAMSTER, SO I CAN SHOVE IT UP MY ANUS. OH HOW I LOVE TO DO THAT!
MR. PRESIDENT, YOU'RE STILL ON THE AIR.

I LOVE YOU MOMMY

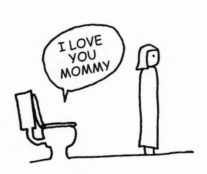

WELL HELLO THERE! NICE TO SEE YOU!
YOU'RE NOT WEARING ANYTHING.

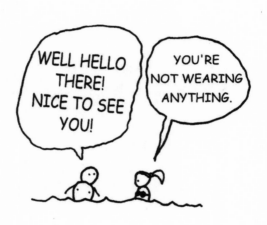

...AND GUESS WHAT! MY KID'S BEING BULLIED AT SCHOOL! BIG TIME! HA HA HA HA HA HA HA HA HA HA HA HA HA HA HA HA HA HA HA HA HA HA HA HA HA... YEAH, I KNOW!

GOOD MORNING KIDS, I'M YOUR NEW TEACHER, AND MY NAME IS MR. SWEATY CUM SEXSEXSEX.

...DO YOU TAKE THIS WOMAN...
SURE! BUT I BETTER GET A BLOWJOB OUT OF THIS! RIGHT GUYS?!

HEY KIDS! LOOK WHAT I FOUND INSIDE YOUR MOMMY!

MY ASS IS BLEEDING

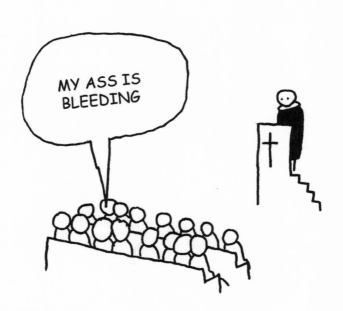

THIS IS MY LOVELY WIFE, BRITNEY
IT'S GWEN

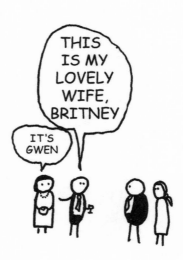

I'M VERY SORRY, BUT YOUR BABY IS DEAD.
MY GABY IS RED? WHAT DOES THAT MEAN?

DADDY? CAN I HAVE YU-GI-OH PYJAMAS FOR CHRIST-MAS?
THAT'S IT...

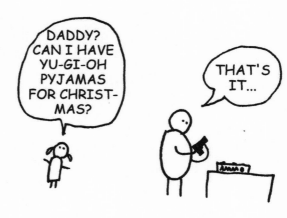

HA HA HA CHECK IT OUT! AN OLD DWARF!
HA HA HA HA HA HA HA HA HA HA I HATE HIM!!

...KIDS... ...DADDY'S HAVING A HEART ATTACK...
HAHAHA HA HA HA HA HAHAHAHA

KIDS!
DINNER!

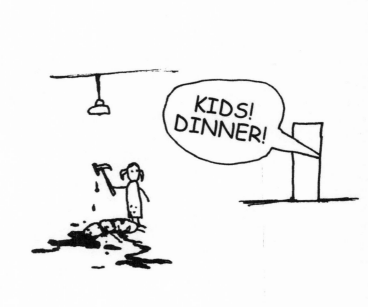

FUCK! FUCK! COCK! PUSSY!
JESUS, DAD! YOU ARE SUCH A DORK!

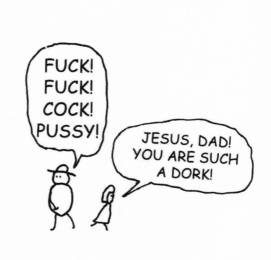

HA HA HA HA !
I AM SHITTING
IN THE SINK!
WC
O

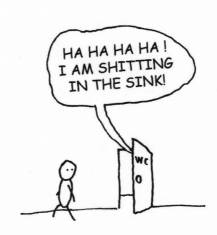

OH, I DON'T KNOW...
COME ON! ALL SAILORS DO IT! I'LL EVEN WEAR A CONDOM!

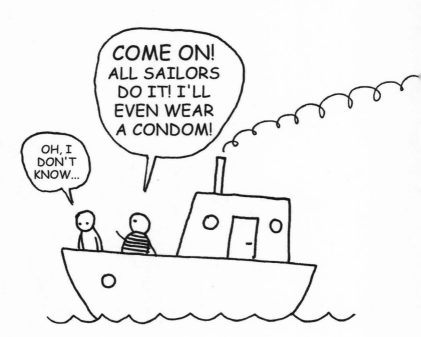

YOU KNOW I'M BAD! YOU KNOW IT...

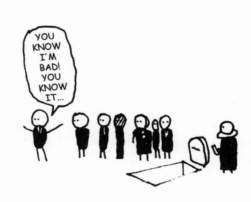

LOOK BERNARD! OUR BABY CAN FLY !!

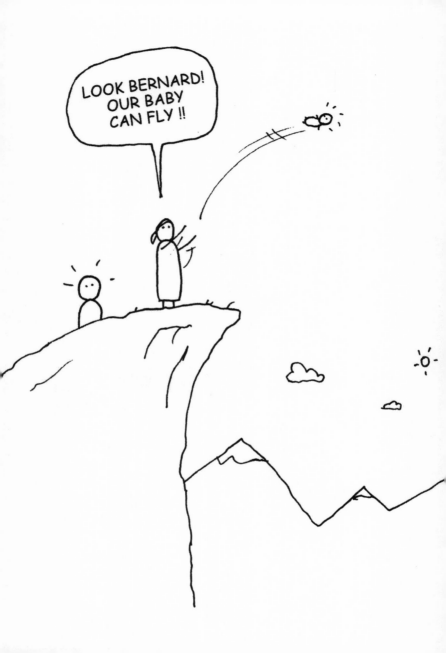

IT SAYS HERE THAT YOU LISTEN TO BOY GEORGE. IS THAT TRUE?
UM... ...NO

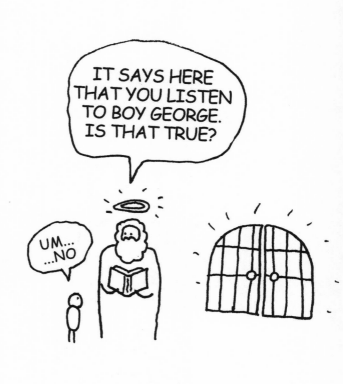

I....
...I LOVE YOU
OH, I KNOW HOW YOU FEEL. BUT I'D RATHER DRINK FIFTY GALLONS OF DOGPISS THAN HAVE SEX WITH YOU, HAROLD.
I'M SORRY...

YOU CHEEKY BASTARD! YOU WANNA FIGHT!?
HMM... WELL, AS LONG AS IT'S SOME SORT OF A LOVE-FIGHT

HAHAHA, WHAT IS HE UP TO NOW?

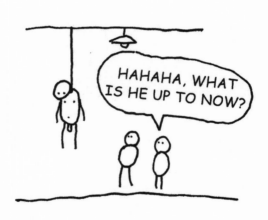

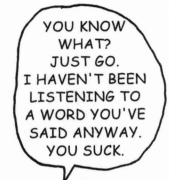

YOU KNOW
WHAT?
JUST GO.
I HAVEN'T BEEN
LISTENING TO
A WORD YOU'VE
SAID ANYWAY.
YOU SUCK.

WHAT'S WRONG?
STEVE. THAT IS NOT A WOMAN.

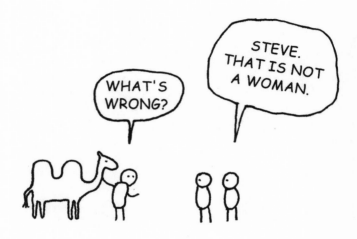

UM...
DO YOU
SELL
CONDOMS?
BLASPHEMER!!!

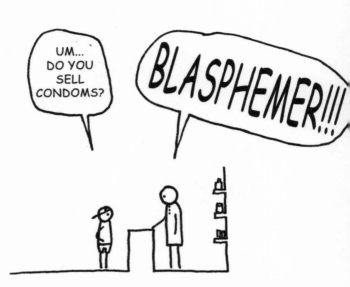

YOU CAN EAT MY PENIS IF I CAN EAT YOURS.

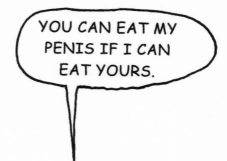

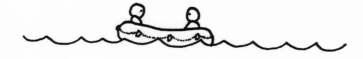

DAMN, I'M DRUNK

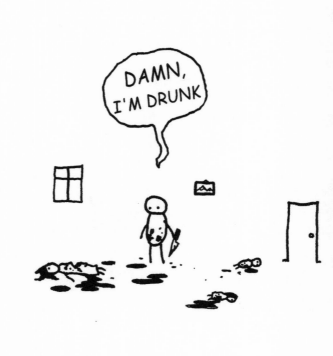

MR. PRESIDENT, WHAT'S THE MATTER?
I HAVE NO FRIENDS

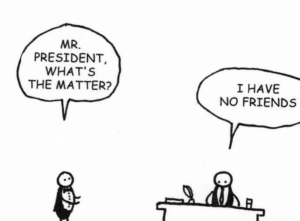

TRUST ME

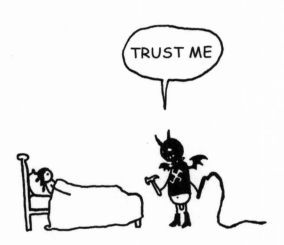

IN A FEW MINUTES YOU'RE GONNA DIE OF SEVERE FOOD POISONING. PLEASE DO IT OUTSIDE. THAT WILL BE FIFTY DOLLARS. THANK YOU.

ALRIGHT,
HEADS: RENT A VIDEO,
TAILS: BUY A HOOKER.

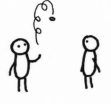

HI

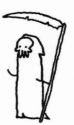

IT'S YOUR FAULT I'M NOT A FAMOUS ROCKSTAR!!
DADDY NO!

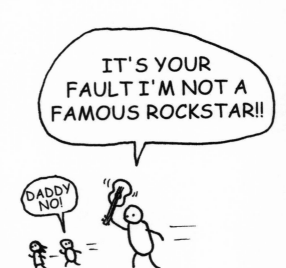

YOU KNOW DAVID, YOU HAVE YOUR FATHER'S EYES
HOW DID YOU KNOW? DID YOU FIND THE BODY?

(SOB) WHO'S ALWAYS SENDING ME DEATH-THREATS?
HEE HEE HEE HEE HEE HEE HEE

HEY! YOU'RE NOT THE DEVIL! YOU'RE LENNY KRAVITZ!

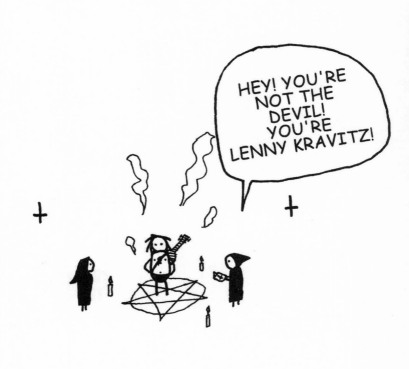

COME OVER HERE SONNY BOY. I WANT TO PISS IN YOUR MOUTH.

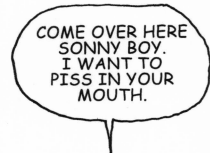

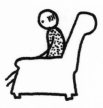

BOB, I'M PREGNANT
HALE FUCKING LUJA

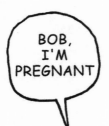

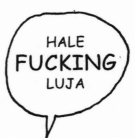

OH COME ON MARCIA! PLEASE FORGIVE ME! I PROMISE I'LL NEVER DO IT AGAIN! I'M SORRY!
DOUGLAS! YOU ATE MY CAT AND PISSED ON MY FACE! AND LAUGHED!

OH HI BRIAN! WHEN IS YOUR WIFE DUE?
IN TWO WEEKS. HERE'S HOPING I'LL BE DEAD BY THEN

WOW.
I AM SO NOT GOING BACK THERE.

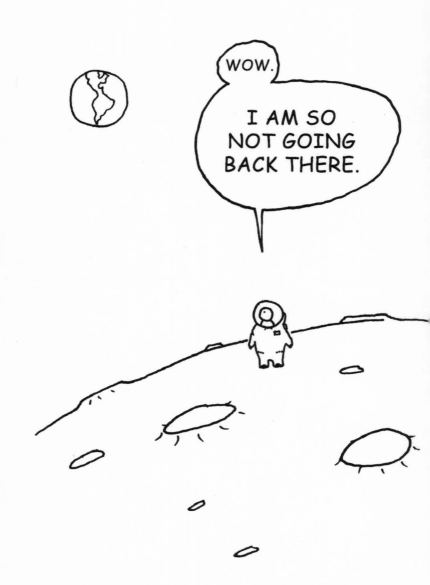

IF I'D HAVE KNOWN YOU WERE SUCH A SHIT IN BED, I NEVER WOULD HAVE MARRIED YOU.

HELLO. ...I AM ANTONIO.
OH! ITALIANS ARE LIKE, SO SEXY!

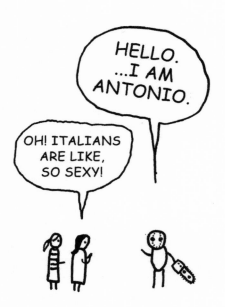

PLEASE GOD... IF YOU COULD JUST GIVE ME SOME SORT OF A SIGN...
JUST JUMP!

WHAT DO YOU WANT FOR CHRISTMAS, KATIE?
FREEDOM

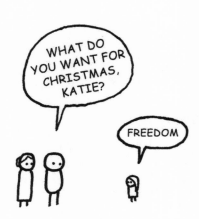

MY CHILDREN SAY THEY DON'T BELIEVE IN GOD ANYMORE FATHER

THAT'S BECAUSE HE'S DEAD. I KILLED HIM MYSELF A FEW DAYS AGO, AND BURIED HIM IN MY BACKYARD.

AAAAHH!! WHAT AM I DOING WRONG?!
YOU'RE HOLDING IT THE WRONG WAY AROUND! AND DON'T SMOKE WITH YOUR EYE!

A SWEATER.
WHY DO YOU HATE ME?

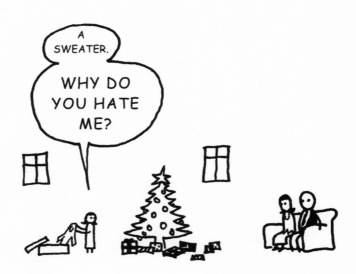

AAAAH! AAAAHH! BEES! MOMMY HELP US!!!
YOU KNOW WHAT? I'D RATHER WATCH.

I LOVE YOU

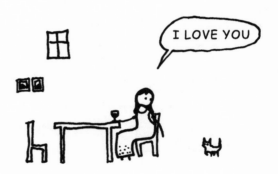

TEE HEE
HEE HEE HEE
HEE HEE!
RETIREMENT
HOME
PETROL

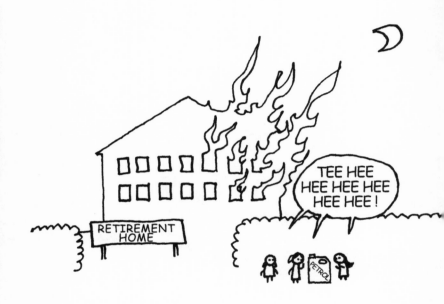

I SMELL DICK.
I JUST FARTED.
HOME SWEET HOME

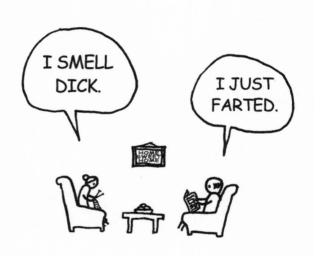

CHECK IT OUT! I CAN PUKE BLOOD AND TALK AT THE SAME TIME!

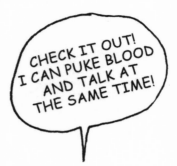

IF YOU CAN'T EVEN MAKE IT ACROSS THE STREET ON YOUR OWN, THEN WHY THE FUCK DID YOU EVEN LEAVE THE FUCKING HOUSE IN THE FIRST PLACE, BITCH??!!!!

...FOR AS IT SAYS IN THE BIBLE...
HEY! THAT'S NOT THE BIBLE! THAT'S THE LATEST HARRY POTTER!!

CUSTOMS
DON'T STOP

LET'S SEE... I HAVE A HOUSE, A CAR AND TWO KIDS.
AMAZING! IT JUST SO HAPPENS THAT I ONCE BURNED DOWN A HOUSE, STOLE A CAR, AND KILLED TWO KIDS!

TAKE ME

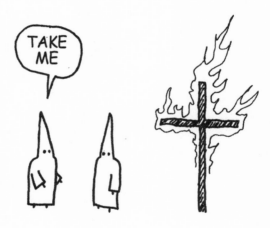

WHAT ARE OUR PARENTS DOING?
FUCKING.
NOW IF YOU'LL EXCUSE ME, I'M GOING TO JUMP OUT THE WINDOW.
AAH
OH

FRANKIE, SAY HELLO TO YOUR NEW DADDY, MALCOLM.
STAR WARS SUCKS AND SANTA CLAUS IS A LIE.

DID I SAY ROUTINE CHECKUP? I MEANT MURDER.

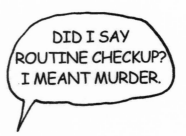

YOU ARE SO BEAUTIFUL, I HATE YOU.

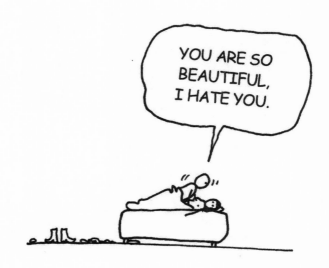

SOMETIMES I DREAM THAT SHARKS LIKE THESE ARE EATING YOU ALIVE.
THEN I WAKE UP LAUGHING.
Aquarium

GUESS WHAT! I JUST WON THE LOTTERY!!!
GUESS WHAT! YOU'RE GONNA DIE A HAPPY MAN!!!

SHIT! THE MAYOR IS COMING!! QUICK, HELEN! HIDE THE RETARD!
I HAVE A NAME.

FUCK ME
rusl

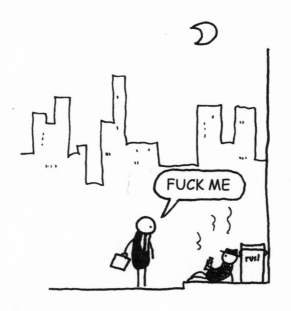

THIS ISN'T CHOCO- LATE PUDDING. THIS IS FAECES.
THEN STOP MAKING ME COOK.

THIS IS YOUR CAPTAIN SPEAKING. I JUST WANT TO TELL YOU THAT I REALLY HATE EVERY SINGLE ONE OF YOU.

DARLING, I THOUGHT I TOLD YOU NOT TO SMOKE YOUR TOBACCO AROUND THE CHILD.
YES YOU DID. BUT YOU FAIL TO REALISE THAT IT IS NOT TOBACCO I AM SMOKING...
...IT'S CRACK.

MOTHER.
FATHER.
I REALLY,
REALLY WANT
TO DIE.

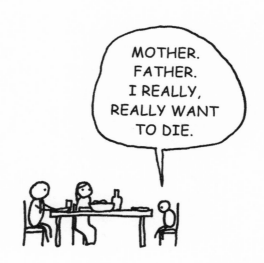

THERE STANDS AN OLD SOUL, WORTHY OF SACRIFICING ON THE ALTAR OF LEVIATHAN.
I COMMEND YOU ON YOUR CHOICE, SIR.

I WET MYSELF

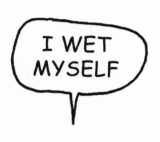

YOU DON'T LOOK SO HOT, CRAIG. ARE YOU FEELING ALRIGHT?
NO. MY WIFE SEWED MY ASSHOLE SHUT THE OTHER DAY. AND NOW I'M FILLING UP WITH POOP.

HMM... WHO SHALL WE BULLY THIS SEMESTER?
YES. WHO INDEED.

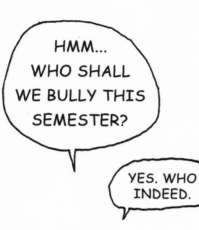

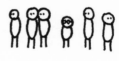

WHEN I GROW UP I'M GONNA BE AS THIN AS YOU, MOMMY.
OF COURSE.

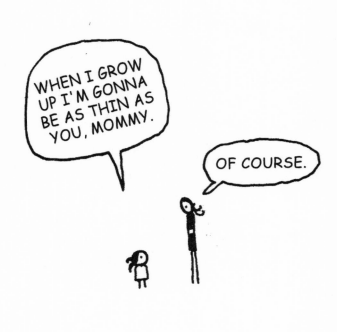

SORRY I'M LATE SWEETY. I HOPE YOU MANAGED TO FIX YOUR DINNER BY YOURSELF.
I ATE A RAT.

OH NO!!
YEAST
INFECTION!!
BLAM!
BLAM!
BLAM!
AAAARHHRHAH

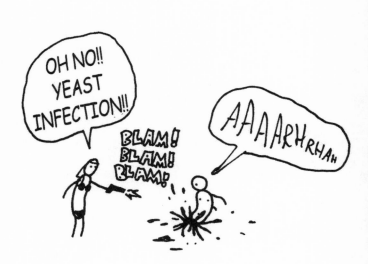

SILENT BUT DEADLY.

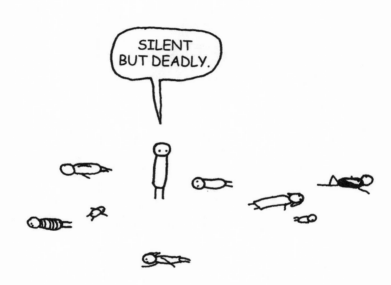

OH MY GOD!! WHAT IS THAT THING?!!
RELAX, IT'S JUST THE GHOST OF MY EX.

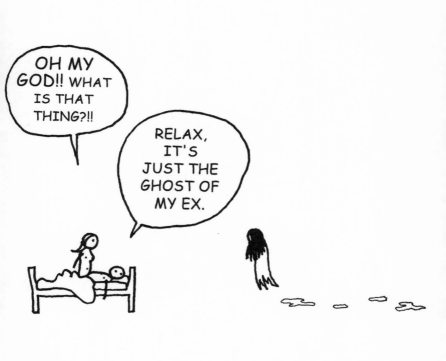

OUCH!!
I SAID NO
BITING!

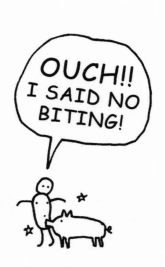

HEIL HITLER
HEIL HITLER
HEIL HITLER

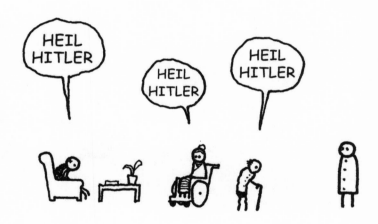

I DON'T KNOW WHETHER I SHOULD LAUGH OR CRY.

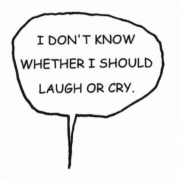

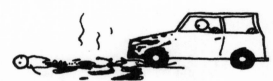

MEOW, I LOVE YOU
THAT'S IT. I'M HAVING IT PUT TO SLEEP!
OK.

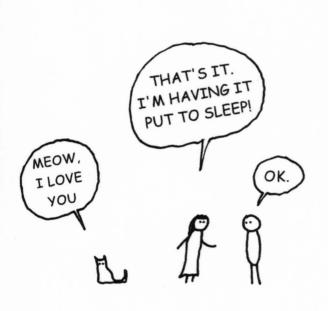

WHAT ARE YOU READING, SAMMY?
OUR DAUGHTER'S DIARY. DID YOU KNOW SHE IS A FILTHY SLUT?

ARE YOU GUYS INTO SWINGING?

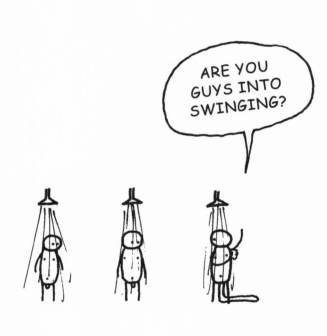

HA HA HA! FOOLED YOU! YOU SEE, I PUT SOME "MAGIC MUSHROOMS" ON THE PIZZA, KIDS!
I'M A DANCING CORPSE!
BLOGHH

HAPPY BIRTHDAY TO YOU, HAPPY BIRTHDAY TO YOU...
I'M WATCHING STAR TREK!

THIS IS MY FATHER, JACK.
AS YOU CAN SEE, HE HAS BREASTS LIKE A WOMAN.
HI.

WHAT'S IT LIKE IN HEAVEN, MOM?
COLD.

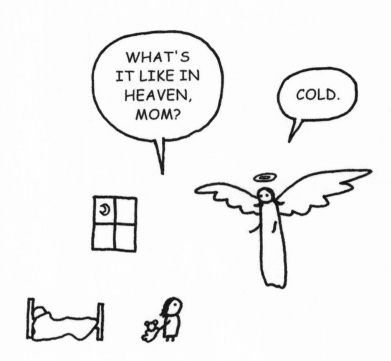

HELLO LITTLE GIRL. ALLOW ME TO INTRODUCE MYSELF. I AM THE DEVIL, AND YOU ARE MY FUTURE WIFE.

FOUR MORE YEARS!! FOUR MORE YEARS!!

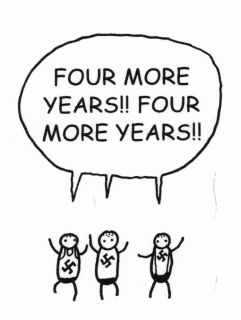

WAIT A MINUTE... THIS ISN'T TENNIS! THIS IS ANAL SEX!!

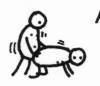

HAHAHA! WHO ARE YOU SUPPOSED TO BE?
YOUR MOTHER.

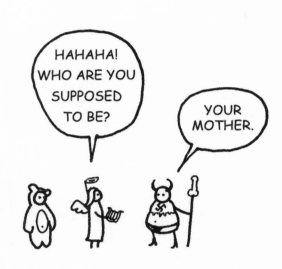

HA HA HA HA! ...WELL NOW YOU KNOW! HOW ABOUT YOU? WHAT'S THE WORST THING YOUV'E EVER DONE?
UM... I ONCE PARTICIPATED IN A GANG-RAPE.

MOOMIN TROLL!
MOOMIN TROLL!
I'M NOT A MOOMIN TROLL!
I JUST HAVE A VERY RARE SYNDROME!

I WANT ONE NIGHT WITH YOUR WOMAN. NO, TWO!
BUT DAD...

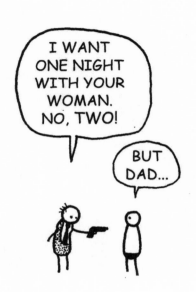

MOMMY, I DRANK SOME PAINT AND NOW I FEEL DIZZY.
THAT'S NICE DEAR.

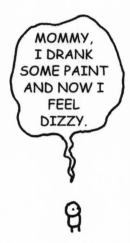

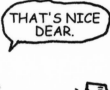

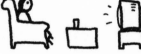

HOW DO YOU DO.
I WAS MASTURBATING

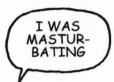

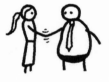

HA HA! KIDS, THERE IS NO REASON TO BE SCARED OF GRANDMA!
AAARRGHH! AAARRHH!

...AND BEFORE I REALISE WHAT'S GOING ON, MY SON HAS GOTTEN HIS HEAD STUCK UP MY ASSHOLE! HA HA HA HA!

WHY ARE YOU CRYING MOM?
I'M CUTTING ONIONS

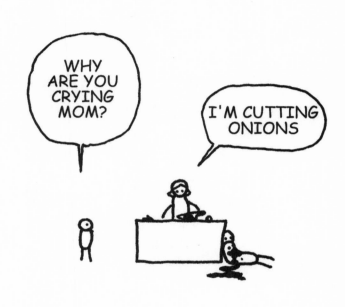

EVERYONE DIES ALONE.

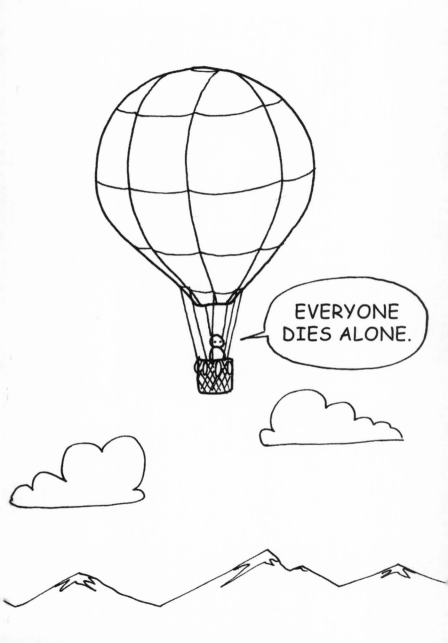

WANNA FUCK HIM?

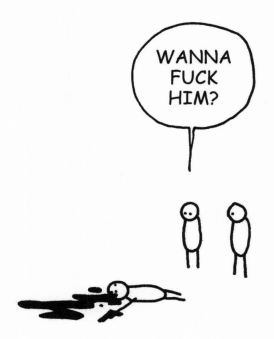

LOOK GUYS! I CUT MY FACE OFF TO PROTEST AGAINST THE WAR!
WAR IS BAD
OIL=BLOOD
FUCK BUSH

LOOK CLOSER IF YOU DARE, AND GAZE UPON...
...THE BEAST WITH TWO BACKS!

I DON'T WANNA BE A DADDY ANYMORE. BYE!

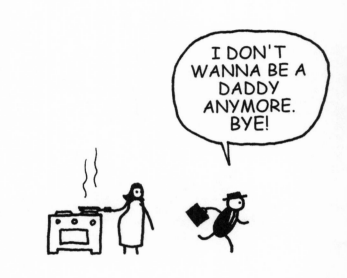

C'MON DAD, FRIENDS IS STARTING! CAN'T YOU JUST ABUSE ME WHEN IT'S OVER?

I'M THE GENIE IN THE BOTTLE. I GRANT YOU ONE WISH.
I WISH TO BECOME A WOMAN.

I MUST BE LOSING MY MIND! I WOKE UP THIS MORNING, WENT TO WORK, BUT FORGOT TO PUT ANY CLOTHES ON!
AMAZING! THE SAME THING HAPPENED TO ME!

OK, HERE'S THE DEAL. I LOVE YOU, BUT IF YOU EVER GET PREGNANT, I'M GONNA STAB YOU TWENTY TIMES IN THE UTERUS.

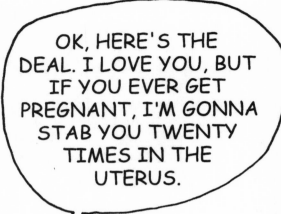

WILL YOU MARRY ME?
YES... OF COURSE YES!
BUT I CAN'T GET MARRIED IN A CHURCH. IT WOULD OFFEND LORD BEELZEBUB.

HERE YOU GO. SCISSORS AND SOME MATCHES. GO PLAY.

10 YEARS OLD!!!
A THONG!! OH THANK YOU MOM AND DAD!

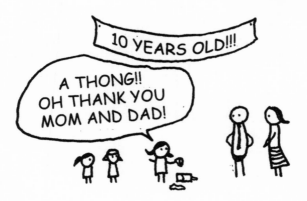

WHY ARE YOU GETTING A DIVORCE?
BECAUSE YOUR FATHER IS A NECRO-PHILIAC.
I CAN'T HELP IT.

ONE FOR BRIDGET JONES.

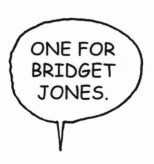

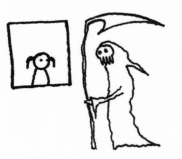

MY NAME IS TOMMY AND I'M AN ALCOHOLIC...
NOT ME! I JUST LOVE LISTENING TO YOU GUYS! FUCKING HILARIOUS!

ARE YOU READY FOR OUR HIGH SCHOOL REUNION, AMY?
LET'S SEE... WALLET... PHONE... KEYS... ANTHRAX... YEAH I'M READY!

I LOVE YOU
AND I YOU

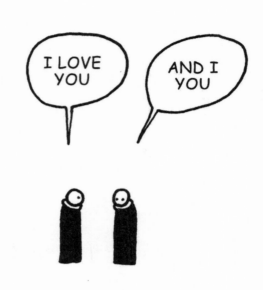

YES THEY'RE IDENTICAL. THE ONLY DIFFERENCE IS THAT BIGBY HAS SEVEN EYES AND CAN SEE INTO THE FUTURE. SOMETIMES HE SPEAKS IN TONGUES.

YOUR BABY IS WEIRD LOOKING.
I SLEPT WITH A HORSE.

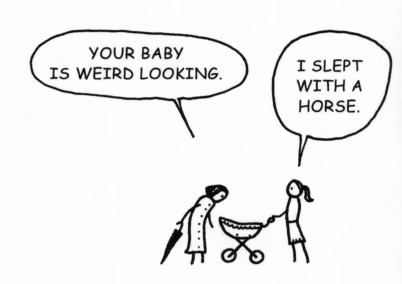

HERE'S TO THE OPPRESSION OF WOMEN!
OPPRESSION OF WOMEN!

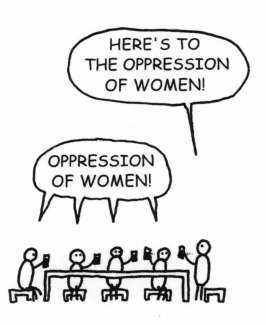

BUT WHAT ABOUT THE CHILDREN? WON'T THEY WAKE UP?
RELAX. I TOOK THE BATTERIES OUT OF THE SMOKE DETECTOR.

SO HOW'S YOUR WIFE?
IT'S NOT A WIFE.
I THINK IT'S SOME KIND OF CON-DENSED EVIL FROM OUTER SPACE.

YOU ARE NO LONGER MY MOTHER. YOU FORGOT TO PICK ME UP.
YOU'RE DEAD TO ME.

I AM SO GAY.
Girls Girls Girls

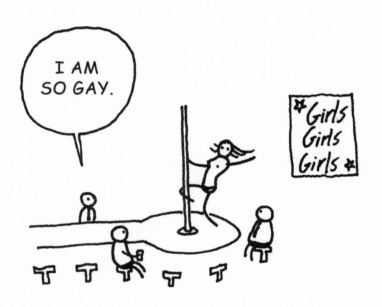

MR. SUMMERS YOU HAVE BEEN FOUND NOT GUILTY OF MURDERING SIX CHILDREN.
WHAT ARE YOU GOING TO DO NOW?
I'M GOING TO DISNEYLAND.

I'LL GIVE YOU 200 BUCKS IF YOU CUT MY HAIR IN THE NUDE.

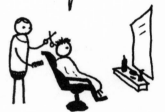

GOOD MORNING MR. WIFEBEATER! I PUT SOMETHING IN YOUR DRINK LAST NIGHT, AND NOW YOUR PENIS IS IN THE SEWER.

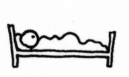

I HATE DOLPHINS. THEY ARE WORSE THAN NAZIS.

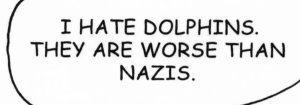

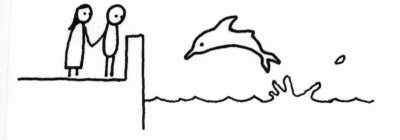

DADDY WHEN I GROW UP I'M GONNA BE A WHORE.
THANKS MTV!

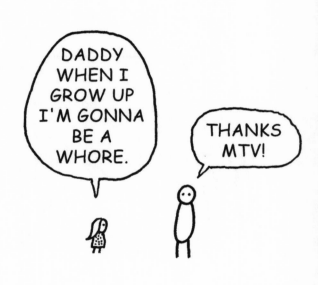

THROW ME OUT THE WINDOW, MOMMY.

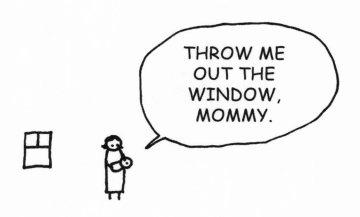

HA HA HA HA HA
HA HA HA HA HA

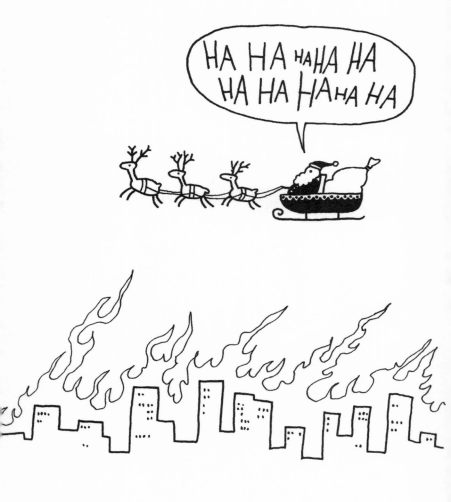

DADDY?
YES?
TELL ME YOU LOVE ME.

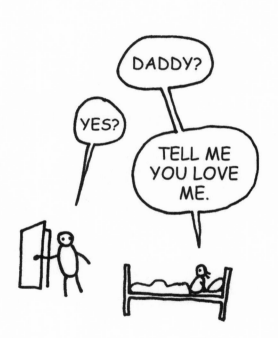

BLEEUGHH!